Sam and his Dad

Robert Loran Floyd

ISBN: 1493625136
ISBN 13: 9781493625130
Library of Congress Control Number: 2013920571
CreateSpace Independent Publishing Platform
North Charleston, South Carolina

This book is for my daughter Ella. You taught me the true meaning of love and continue to inspire me every day. You've blessed my world and you bring a smile to my face every time I see you. I am proud to be your Dad!

It was early on Saturday as Sam
began to rise. He hurried downstairs
with excitement in his eyes.

He yelled for his father, who was
hardly awake, "We're going to miss
our tee time, for goodness sake!"

His mom made them breakfast
as Sam tried to wait, all the time
worrying that they would be late.

His dad finished his coffee, and Sam
ate his eggs. A rush of excitement
ran through his legs.

See, Sam was a small boy, the smallest
in his class. And he couldn't catch
a ball or even throw a pass.

He always was lonely as his
classmates would play. Hoping he'd
grow and be like them one day.

But Saturdays were different; he felt big
and tall. Because his dad always took
him to play the greatest game of all.

He didn't need teammates or a field or a goal.
Just a little white ball, some clubs, and a hole.

So he kissed his mom bye and got in the car.
And hoped that today he'd make his first par.

His dad started the engine, and they
began to drive. Sam's heart was
pounding, and his body felt alive.

His dad smiled softly as they drove
down the street. Sam placed his golf
shoes on his tiny, little feet.

The weather was awesome; the skies were so blue.
The grass had a trace of warm summer dew.

The birds sang sweetly, and the wind
touched the trees. The flowers were bright
as they danced with the bees.

Sam was so happy as they drove through the gate. As
his dad said softly, "I told you we wouldn't be late."

They parked in their spot next to a tree. And
Sam jumped out, his face filled with glee.

They grabbed their clubs and walked up the hill. His
dad whispered something to the starter named Bill.

Sam said hello to all the people he saw.
And never before did he feel so tall.

Everyone knew him; they called him by name. They
smiled and they nodded as Sam did the same.

They walked through the clubhouse like
many before, and straight toward the
first tee—right through the door.

The pro was outside as they walked down the path.
And the birds made the fountain their personal bath.

Sam walked clumsily with his bag on his back.
His dad grabbed some balls out of his sack.

They got to the first tee and set their
bags on the ground. And Sam saw the
people that had gathered around.

See, everyone there realized Sam
was so small. But they all loved to
watch him hit that first ball.

Now Sam felt some jitters; he felt weak
in the knees. His hand was shaking
as he put the ball on the tee.

He slowly stood up and backed a step away.
He was ready to hit the first shot of the day.

He wiggled his feet and curled up his toes.
He said to himself, "OK, here it goes."

He pulled back the driver with all of
his will. As his dad watched anxiously
with the starter named Bill.

He swung toward the ball with all of his might.
The people all watched this amazing sight.

The ball went flying straight off of that tee.
Right in the fairway for everyone to see.

His dad said, "Good shot," and the
applause lasted a while. Sam turned
around with an ear-to-ear smile.

His dad hit his tee shot and out of
sight they walked. As some members
gathered and some of them talked.

They wondered how Sam could hit it so far. He hoped that today he would make his first par.

Sam thanked his father, as he walked toward his ball, for making this Saturday the best day of all.

Sam hit his second shot up toward the green. But it found the sand that was lying between.

He blasted it out for shot number three. On the first hole no par would there be.

He continued to try; he never gave up. As shot number six hit the bottom of the cup.

He admired his dad as his dad made his par.
He hoped that one day he could hit it that far.

They walked off the green, father
and son. Sam wrote "six" on the
scorecard under hole number one.

They played the next few holes, and
Sam played them fine. But his search
for a par was still on his mind.

Then came hole number five, the
shortest par three of them all. Sam
stood up and whacked at the ball.

Straight for the pin, but was it enough? It fell
barely short; the ball stopped in the rough.

Sam hurried toward it; this might
be his best try. Only thirty feet
from the hole did his ball lie.

As he put his bag down and his club
by the ball. The ball moved ever
so slightly but hardly at all.

Sam looked at his dad, but his dad
turned his head. As the question of
honor ran thru Sam's head.

He then chipped the ball so close
to the pin. And walked with his
putter and then tapped it in.

His ball had moved but no one could see.
Had Sam really made his very first three?

He got out his scorecard to write down
the score. To his dad's amazement,
Sam wrote down a "four."

Sam's dad was confused; how could
it be? As he counted Sam's shots, he
asked, "Didn't you make a three?"

Sam answered softly with tears in his eyes.
"You taught me early to never tell lies."

Sam continued to talk with an obvious
frown. He explained what had happened
when he put his club down.

"My ball moved so slightly, but it
moved because of me. It wouldn't be
right if I wrote down a three."

His dad was so proud he put his
arms around his son. He admired so
deeply what Sam had just done.

"Don't be sad, Sam, you did the right thing.
I'm proud of you, son, for the honor you bring."

Sam was still shaken as they headed to the
next tee. Maybe today wasn't meant to be.

He'd never been so close, so close to his
goal. Of making a par—a par for the hole.

So he and his dad, they played on some more.
Sam never came close to making a four.

They enjoyed the walk and the air
from the breeze. They enjoyed their
talk and the birds and the trees.

Sam enjoyed his time he spent
with his dad. And with the decision
he'd made he didn't feel sad.

So they headed to eighteen, another
par three. The members were
gathering under a large tree.

Sam was a bit tired, and it was
getting hot. But he gathered the
courage to hit one more shot.

He teed up the ball like each time before. But
this time was different; he felt something more.

A burst of energy ran through his
hands. He looked at the green where
he hoped his ball would land.

He pulled back the club again with
a sway. He knew this was the last
hole until next Saturday.

And as he made contact, it felt so sweet. Like
the honey of a bee or the sugar we eat.

As Sam looked up to the blue, blue sky, he
saw the white ball fly ever so high.

It seemed like slow motion as it went through the
air. And he noticed the people who began to stare.

The ball kept going straight through the day.
Would it make the green? Could it find a way?

Straight over the water and left of the sand. On the
front of the green Sam watched the ball land.

And what happened next you'll never believe.
And Sam wouldn't either had he not seen.

The ball bounced forward and rolled toward the pin. And people began standing...could it go in?

It rolled a little farther; boy, this was fun. As the ball disappeared in the hole...Sam made a one!

He fell to the ground, not believing his eyes. He was ever so grateful for golf's greatest prize.

The people were yelling; his dad's eyes filled with tears. For he never had made one in all of his years.

Sam ran toward his dad and into his arms, proud, as laughter and joy burst through the crowd.

Sam never will forget that day; neither will I, as I couldn't help looking up into the sky.

Sam had a choice way back on number five. He did the right thing when he could have lied.

A couple hours later was much more fun. As life repaid Sam with his first hole in one.